BIMBO.TV OMNIBUS

SADIE THATCHER

CONTENTS

1

BIMBO VISION

"Come on," Beatrice grunted as she pushed the box through the front door of her apartment. She was only vaguely aware that she had won a contest, something online that she barely remembered entering. But she had won and that meant she had just received a brand new television.

Beatrice had just returned home from work when she found the waiting package outside her door. She was already tired, finding her office job exhausting. There were so many proverbial fires she had to put out each day that she never came home with any energy left. And it had been awkward pushing the box into her apartment while still wearing her business outfit. The low heels and beyond knee-length skirt made such efforts difficult. The suit jacket only made it worse, keeping her body heat in.

By the time the door closed, Beatrice looked even more haggard than usual after a day of work. Even if she wanted to go out, she was too tired.

Leaving the television box by the door, Beatrice walked into her bedroom so that she could change out of her work clothes. She kicked off her heels, disliking how they made her feet hurt at the end of the day. However, there were certain fashion constructs that required her to wear them. That was not to say that Beatrice disliked heels entirely. She had experimented with wearing taller heels on the rare occasions she went out, but it was hard for her to manage the energy when there always seemed to be so much else she needed to do.

Beatrice shrugged off the jacket and hung it up in her closet. Then she carefully unbuttoned her plain white blouse to reveal the plain white bra she wore underneath. There were times when she wondered why she even bothered with bras. But again, like with the heels, she understood the convention that required it. It was one more burden she put up with to fit in.

The skirt followed, sliding it over her hips and then down her legs to reveal her plain white panties. Beatrice hung up the skirt, not knowing when she would wear it again or if it would need to go to the cleaners first. She then stepped into the bathroom so she could let her dark hair out of the bun she kept it in during the workday and instead put it in a ponytail.

Beatrice lived a simple life, one that largely revolved around her job. What little energy she had left was just enough to keep her apartment clean. The few friends she had, which were closer to acquaintances, would have described Beatrice as a stick in the mud. She would have agreed with them.

It was only after Beatrice had changed into a comfy pair of sweatpants and a baggy top that she turned her attention to how she was going to spend the rest of her evening. It was Friday night and many people were headed out. Beatrice had actually been invited to a happy hour function with a few coworkers, but she had shrugged it off, apologizing for being too tired. That was mostly true. She was too tired to go out and try to be social.

First up was eating. Beatrice pulled a meal out of the freezer and tossed it into the microwave, not feeling up to cooking. That was a normal situation for her. She was not a natural cook and she rarely had the energy to do more than press a couple buttons on the microwave. But once her dinner was spinning away in the microwave, she turned her attention to her new television.

The box looked intimidating. The television was big, likely making it awkward to move. It had been hard enough just getting it over the threshold of her apartment. But then she looked at her old television. It was an early flat panel model that had clearly seen better days. It was still functional, but it did not have any of the functionality of a modern smart television. It could not even connect to the internet if Beatrice wanted it to.

Not wanting to wait, Beatrice managed to open the box before her meal finished cooking. She pulled out the setup instructions so she could read about her new television while she ate. It quickly became apparent to her that the new television was not just modern, but it was state of the art. The contest she won did not just send her a random model that had been sitting on a shelf somewhere. This had top of the line picture and sound quality. Beatrice wondered how loud she would be able to turn it up, not wanting to disturb her neighbors.

However, even though Beatrice was tired and she wanted nothing more than to curl up on the couch and watch a documentary or read a book, she decided she needed to set the new television up and figure out how it worked. That took precedence over rest and relaxation. Once it was ready to go, she could put a movie on and fall asleep on the couch if she wanted to.

The setup for the television was easy. The whole thing was plug and play. All she had to do was replace her old television on her entertainment center with the new one and plug it in. The old television went into the box so she could eventually get rid of it, assuming the new one worked for her. She still needed to test it out.

As soon as the remote was in Beatrice's hands, she shivered as a burst of pleasure traveled down her spine. That had been unexpected, but she did not connect it to anything. And it was soon forgotten as she turned on the television for the first time.

The screen lit up with a pink graphic depicting a cartoon television. "Welcome to Bimbo dot TV," a seductive woman's voice said. The sound practically wrapped around Beatrice as she sat on her couch, caressing her and helping ease the tension she still felt from her workday. She had never heard of this brand of television before, but Beatrice was not someone who kept up with the latest technology trends. That was why she had such an old television to begin with. She had never cared that much before, even if she could use an upgrade.

Once the opening graphic faded, she was prompted to enter a few details about herself. She assumed the television was creating a profile for her. Beatrice had no problem providing her age and gender. She had never been very careful about protecting her data. And once she had created her profile, the final step was to enter her WiFi password.

Beatrice felt overwhelmed as she looked at the home screen. She did not know what to do. She could download apps to use or just flip to a regular channel. She was not sure which she should do. However, the television came with one app already installed. It was called Bimbo.TV, matching the brand of the television. Not knowing what else to do, she decided to see what kind of content the native app came with.

The moment the app launched, Beatrice was inundated with light and sound. She sat up straight, her eyes looking like a deer that had gotten caught in the headlights of an oncoming car. Without blinking, she stared straight ahead as the pink screen began to rotate in a spiral.

The trance that sucked Beatrice down was almost instantaneous. One moment she had been completely alert and looking forward to exploring new content on her new television and the next her mind was an almost complete blank. No thoughts managed to make it through the molasses that was her gray matter. It was almost like the Beatrice that had once been had been zapped away in a wave of light and sound.

The words flowing out of the television filled Beatrice's mind, giving her new and foreign thoughts that were indistinguishable from her own.

"I feel good."

"I love to watch the spiral."

"No thoughts are the best thoughts."

"Listen and obey."

The mantras varied. Some repeated, others only needed to be said once. Some Beatrice even started to repeat when she heard them, her voice slow and flat, her body little more than a drone repeating instructions.

However, while the voice and spiral inundated Beatrice's mind, filling her with new ideas and new ways of thinking, the television had another purpose, one that it was specially designed to do. The room filled with an ethereal pink light, focusing on Beatrice, almost making her glow. This glow did not originate from the screen, but from something deeper inside the machine. For the Bimbo.TV television was more than just a screen to watch, but a device that could transform the viewer in mind and in body.

As Beatrice's body glowed, her clothing faded away, simply disappearing, leaving her completely nude. But with her in trance, she felt nothing. She had no awareness that her clothing had disappeared. She had no awareness of the warm air flowing over her skin.

But it was that pink glow that was responsible for not only Beatrice's clothes disappearing, but for the transformation of her body. It started simply. As she sat there, her body became long and lean, giving her new height. She would be tall without ever being too tall.

However, that was only the foundation for Beatrice's new body. From the inside out, she was remade. Her waist tightened, her insides rearranging themselves to better fit her new proportions. Next came the widening of her hips, giving her a base from which the rest of her hourglass figure would be built upon.

And Beatrice was about to be graced with an hourglass figure that few could rival. That was because as her legs gained tone to match her waist, her breasts began to balloon up off her chest. The days of her being almost flat chested were over. They started small, simply shifting in proportion, losing their teardrop shape and becoming more round. But that sizing was short lived, because they soon began to inflate, just like two balloons hooked up to an air compressor.

Her boobs were not the only part of her that inflated either. Her ass bubbled up underneath her, mostly hidden by the cushions of the couch she sat on. But once she stood, she would have a bubble butt that rivaled the size of her boobs, making sure that there was always some part of her body to draw in the eye.

As Beatrice's breasts grew into a pair of fake boobs and

then into territory where it was more appropriate to call them tits, other parts of her new body took shape. Her eyes, having previously been a slate gray, moved on the color spectrum until they were a bright blue, almost glowing in the same way that her body glowed with the pink light that infused every inch of her apartment.

But it was not just her eyes that changed on her face. Her nose slimmed and turned up ever so slightly at the end, giving her a cute button nose. Her cheeks filled out, her cheekbones becoming more prominent as she gained a heart-shaped complexion. Yet it was her lips that would forever draw attention. It started small, much like how her breasts started to expand. Her lips started to look a little puffier, as if she had naturally full lips.

Except that Beatrice's new form was not one that was subtle. Naturally full was not good enough so they continued to grow, pushing out from her face, gaining in both volume and in projection. It was not long until her lips formed a natural O-shape, and everyone who saw her would think her lips had a single purpose. Beatrice had lips designed for cocksucking.

And just as her lips finished growing, so too did Beatrice's tits. They were big and round, far bigger than was natural. Given their roundness, that had to be assumed. They were fake tits and everyone who saw them would know that. There was no hiding them, even if her tiny pink nipples were not always visible. Not even a thick sweater would be enough to hide her new size. Even wearing coveralls would still leave people looking at her chest, knowing their unnatural size, even if their shape was hidden from view.

Beatrice's hourglass figure was complete, but her final look was far from finished. Pink appeared on her nails, both toes and fingers. The work was perfect and clearly came at the hands of a professional. And that became even more clear once her fingernails reached a glamor length that would make many handheld tasks difficult, if not impossible. Her typing days were over, even if her mind was in a condition where typing could still be expected of her.

With her hands complete, a deep tan began to spread over Beatrice's skin. And as the darker coloring flowed over her like paint flowing over her, every blemish on her skin simply disappeared. By the time the coloring reached the top of her head, Beatrice had completely smooth skin without a mark or even a hair growing anywhere below her neck. And even above her neck, the hair was limited to carefully sculpted eyebrows and thick and full lashes to frame her wide eyes.

However, there was still one physical part of Beatrice's body that needed changing to fit with her new image. Her dark hair disappeared from her head, leaving her momentarily bald. But that was only so that new hair follicles could grow and develop, giving her a new and more vibrant shade of hair, not to mention increased volume and improved texture.

When Beatrice's new hair sprouted, it came out platinum blonde in color, looking entirely fake, but completely natural for her new body. It contrasted perfectly with her tanned skin. But it was not enough to just change the color and volume. Length was key. Beatrice's hair grew and grew, framing her heart-shaped face until it ran down her back, all the way to her ass, and pooled on top of her tits in loose waves, a look that appeared natural, but actually required hours of preparation to get right.

One look at the new Beatrice and it was immediately obvious that she was a bimbo. Porn star might have been the other description, but that was just par for the course with a body that had been so clearly designed to make cocks hard and then to be fucked by them.

With Beatrice's new body complete, the rest of her life

needed an upgrade. The pink glow from the television invaded every inch of the apartment, transforming her furniture from the old and beat up pieces that had served her well since her college days into something more modern and chic. Pink continued to be a primary theme, matching her pink lips and her pink nails. Even Beatrice's wardrobe was transformed, giving her an array of outfits to choose from that both fit her new body and that were designed to highlight her new features.

Nothing about Beatrice's apartment would connect to the old her. Her past had all but been erased, left to be just a few disjointed memories, and only when she needed them to remember who people were or how to get around town.

But with all of that done, there was still one last physical change to make. Beatrice needed new clothing. Her old baggy top and sweatpants simply would not cut it for a woman of artificial beauty. She needed something that would both fit her, but also display her body to best effect. It started with heels. Where Beatrice had stuck to low heels of maybe an inch, occasionally experimenting with something in the two-inch variety, the new Beatrice was someone with an eye for fashion and impossibly tall heels.

The pink sandals that appeared on her feet, making sure to keep her pink painted toenails visible, featured a heel of around six inches and a platform beneath the toe that would make it looked like Beatrice was always standing on a pedestal. And even though she had never worn heels that high before, her new body was perfectly designed for it, able to find a perfect balance while walking with cat-like grace.

The final component of her outfit was a dress. The halter-style dress featured a plunging neckline that dipped nearly to her belly-button, leaving both her back bare and her tits barely covered by the sparkly pink material. And once the fabric all came together to form the skirt portion of the dress, it was barely long enough to keep her ass cover. Bending over would make it clear she was not wearing any panties. And in just the right light, her dress would shine like a disco ball, reflecting light around her, all of it tinted pink.

And while all of this was going on, Beatrice's mind was bombarded with both overt signals in the form of mantras that accompanied the spiraling visual effects on the screen. But it was the subliminal messages that were the real game changers. They helped instigate the rewiring of Beatrice's brain, transitioning her mind away from complex ideas and narrowing her focus to that which her body was now best suited for. Sex now lived at the forefront of Beatrice's mind. She dressed for sex, highlighting her body to best effect.

However, there was more to it than just turning her mind toward sex. Her mind needed to be programmed for everything that she had missed in her life before. It was a mental transformation that gave her a genius-level expertise in how to use her body, how to turn people on, how to get them off. And her in the process.

But the final change happened right at the end. When the pink glow stopped, when the spiral slowed to a stop, when the voice helping to teach her the new mantras that would forevermore define her life ended, there was one part of her that needed to be done away with so that she could live her best bimbo life. Her name needed to go.

When she came out of her trance, she sat there in complete bliss, not remembering what she had been doing and completely oblivious to the transformation she had undergone. When she looked down and was greeted with her impressive cleavage for the first time, she reached up and grabbed them with her long nailed fingers, enjoying their large size and the pleasurable sensations that ran through her, especially when her fingers pinched her nipples. She shuddered with pleasure as a jolt traveled down her spine, making her already wet pussy gush.

"Bebe loves her big titties," she said, using her new name for the first time. But it was not just her name that had changed. Her whole style of speech had shifted, along with her voice rising at least one octave, making sure she always sounded like the bimbo she now was.

Before Bebe could get too involved in exploring her new body, even if she had no concept that it was new to her, the doorbell rang.

"Bebe is coming," she called out as she pushed herself up from the couch and tugged at the hem of her dress, making sure that it remained long enough to cover her ass. With her new fashion sense, that would always be a battle and not always one that she would win.

Bebe swayed her hips as she moved across the room toward the door. While her furniture and decor fit with her new bimbo life, her apartment still had the same floor plan that it had before. It was a simple one-bedroom apartment with an interior hallway that connected the different units in the building.

When Bebe reached the door, she looked through the peephole, having to bend slightly to do so. Beatrice would have had to push herself up onto her tiptoes, but Bebe bent slightly at the waist, letting her large tits dangle in front of her as she looked through the tiny hole.

Bebe's first thought when she saw the figure standing on the other side of the door was simply that it was a man. She bounced with excitement, her tits jiggling unrestrained beneath the fabric of her dress. But then she realized that the man was her neighbor, Isaac. He lived directly across the hall from her.

Bebe threw open the door and posed herself in the doorway, one hand on her hip and the other on the doorframe.

"Hey there, stud," she said before she licked her lips. Every part of Bebe's appearance expressed her lust. Her hooded eyes, her suggestive pose, even the way her eyes naturally dropped toward Isaac's crotch, hopeful that she might find what he was packing there.

"Beatrice?" Issac said, unsure of what he was seeing. The woman before him looked nothing like the neighbor he barely knew and only saw occasionally. But there were enough similarities for him to guess that this vision of bimbo beauty was his neighbor.

Bebe giggled before she answered. "Call me Bebe."

"Yeah, okay, Bebe," Isaac said, swallowing hard as sweat broke out on his brow. He was not used to talking to a woman like this. His eyes traveled up and down her body, trying not to stare at any one feature for too long. Not that it was easy. The way Bebe's tits were on display made it hard for him to concentrate on anything else.

"What can Bebe do for you?" she finally prompted. She eyed the growing tent in his pants and licked her lips at the mere idea of taking a taste.

"Oh, right," Isaac said, pulling his attention back to his reason for ringing her doorbell to begin with. "I saw there was a package outside your door earlier and then it was gone. I wanted to make sure you knew about it and got it."

"That's, like, so sweet," Bebe gushed. "But Bebe totes got it. She won a new TV and it's super cool. Do you want to come in and see it? Bebe would love to show it to you."

Speaking largely in the third person was a completely new experience for the newly formed bimbo, but she could not think of any other way to speak. Referring to herself as Bebe simply made sense to her. The ability to refer to herself in any other way had been reduced to moments when it was impossible to speak in the third person. Not that Bebe actually noticed this. She barely noticed anything beyond the tent in Isaac's pants. Isaac, however, did notice and responded with a growing lust for his now incredibly sexy next-door neighbor.

"Um, yeah, sure," Isaac said, not entirely sure what he was getting himself into, but unwilling to shut the door on his bimbo of a neighbor. She looked far too good to him to consider walking away from her.

Bebe beckoned Isaac into her apartment, using a long-nailed finger to coax him to follow her. And he followers her like a moth drawn to a flame, his eyes fixating on her exposed cleavage. Bebe added a little shimmy to her shoulders to make her tits jiggle. She giggled at the fact she now had a man in her apartment. There were so many things she wanted to do with him, to let him do to her.

When they reached the couch, Bebe turned and picked up the remote. She stared at it for a moment, trying to remember how to use it. So much of the world was so confusing to her now. Her brain had been repurposed for other things. But it meant she could look on with wonder at the world around her, maintaining a constant sense of surprise. Finally, however, she managed to find the button to turn on the television.

"Welcome to Bimbo dot TV," the sexy voice said. A moment later the main screen appeared and Bebe selected the Bimbo.TV app. It was still the only app available. She would need to download other apps if she wanted to use the full functionality of the television. However, given the power the Bimbo.TV app had over her, she saw little reason to add anything else.

As soon as the spiral appeared, Bebe's face went slack and her eyes opened wide, taking all of it in. There was no ethereal pink glow this time. It was just a spiral with subliminal messages that reinforced Bebe's new way of thinking. She was just a brainless bimbo now, focused on looking and acting as sexy as possible. Nothing else mattered to her.

Isaac, on the other hand, did not see the spiral. Through some technological marvel, the television could project different images to different people, even when they stood right next to each other. While Bebe saw the familiar smile and continued to receive her bimbo programming, Isaac saw something far more fun. He watched as three bimbos, similar in appearance and disposition to Bebe, frolicked on the beach, only wearing skimpy bikinis that covered little and provided even less support.

"You like watching this?" Isaac asked, slightly stunned by his neighbor's choice in television. However, he had no idea that she saw something different. All he knew was that he could sit back and watch a bevy of bimbos play and frolic like that anytime.

"Oh yeah," Bebe said, her voice coming out as a moan. Her already high arousal levels spiked as the subliminal messages she received amped up her already high libido. "Can Bebe sit on your lap while she watches?"

It was a question, but Bebe had already started to push Isaac down onto the couch. As soon as he was seated, she turned away from the television and bent low, giving Isaac a great view of her tits as they were barely restrained by her shimmering dress. She reached out with long-nailed fingers and deftly opened Isaac's pants, freeing his cock. His hard shaft bobbed into view, standing straight up from the impressive blood flow her body created.

When Bebe sat down on Isaac's lap, she did so carefully, guiding his cock toward her pussy, her dress easily riding up and staying out of the way. The moment her folds enveloped him, they both let out a loud moan, unable to keep themselves quiet. The television continued to play and both Isaac and Bebe found themselves watching as Bebe bucked and bounced on Isaac's lap, fucking herself on his meaty cock.

For Bebe, the spiral took up all of her vision. She simply stared at the screen, letting her mind go blank, her body acting on instinct as she fucked her neighbor. For Isaac, it was like watching soft-core porn while Bebe bounced on his cock. The only thing that made it better was when he reached up and started to play with her big tits. Bebe's dress provided no real barrier to his hands. He easily pushed the flimsy fabric aside, letting his hands and fingers probe her new curves.

In any other situation, Bebe's eyes would have rolled up in the back of her head as the pleasure hit her. She had never felt this good, but she had never had a body designed for sex before. However, the spiral on the screen drew in her gaze and prevented her body from reacting too strongly to the pleasure that now coursed through her veins. Her mind had already been bimbofied, but there was no harm in continuing to reinforce those lessons, making sure that her mind never reverted back to its previous form.

"Fuck, you're a hot slut," Isaac groaned as he felt himself nearing his point of no return. He had never imagined sex like this before, but he was certain that Bebe was going to be a frequent part of his life from now on.

"Bebe is a bimbo slut," she responded. It was unclear if she said those words from the television's urging or if it was a natural reaction to Isaac's comment.

Either way, Bebe's confession was enough to push Isaac over the edge. His cock surged with cum as Bebe's own orgasm was triggered. She finally closed her eyes as a flood of erotic pleasure shot through her body. Her orgasm hit her like an explosion, rising up from her pussy and filling every inch of her body. She cried out as her body became flush with pleasure. Her hands came up to grab her tits, but she ended up grabbing Isaac's hands instead, holding his hands on her tits as she continued to roll through her orgasm.

Bebe and Isaac stayed that way for a long time. When Bebe had finally recovered enough from her orgasm to open her eyes again, they once again fixated on the spiral on the screen, letting herself soak in the subliminal messages that now governed her life. There were no longer any thoughts in her head that the television had not put there. There was no more Beatrice. There was only Bebe, the happy and sexy bimbo.

Isaac was happy to simply sit there, his cock still enveloped by Bebe's slick folds. She moved just enough to help reduce his refractory period, making it so he could fuck her all over again when he was ready.

The pair watched the Bimbo.TV app for the next several hours, going late into the night, fucking as often as was possible. Bebe loved it. She had never felt so good before. Every orgasm seemed better than the last, more powerful, more all-encompassing. They seared away any remaining thoughts that might have still been left after the television app purged everything else from her mind.

"I think that's enough of jiggly bimbos for now," Isaac said as he finally turned off the television. He had finally reached his end point for the night. His cock needed rest and maybe an icepack. He had never experienced such a marathon sex session before, but he was also excited to do this again.

"But Bebe totes likes watching that." She pouted, pursing her lips and making them look even bigger. Isaac's cock made a half-hearted attempt to get hard again as he imagined those lips wrapped around his cock. But that would have to wait for another time.

"I want to ask you something, Bebe," Isaac said as he lifted the bimbo off his lap. She made no move to cover herself as she sat back down beside him, their bodies turned toward each other. Her dress was hiked up around her waist and the flimsy straps that had once covered her tits were both pushed to the side, hugging the outside of her tits and forcing them together in an even deeper line of cleavage.

Bebe looked at Isaac, waiting. Her mind was blissfully blank. She would have smiled, but after such a long session with the Bimbo.TV subliminal messages playing through her mind, she could not even draw on the emotion to make that happen. She was happy, but she struggled to express it with such an empty head.

Isaac swallowed hard as he tried to look Bebe in the eyes. His gaze kept trying to fall to her tits. And the way she pushed her chest out did not help his efforts, but he managed. "How about you become my girlfriend?"

Bebe tilted her head, making her look even dumber, but also cuter as she tried to consider Isaac's proposal. She placed a finger at the corner of her mouth as she tried to think. However, her mind remained blank. It was so hard to think. It was no fun. But Isaac seemed like a smart guy and he fucked her really good. Was that enough?

"Does that mean you can fuck me more?" Bebe asked. She had a one track mind now. Her life was all about sex and being sexy.

"Not right now, but tomorrow and every day after that."

"Okay, Bebe will be your girlfriend."

Isaac smiled, unable to believe his luck. He had no idea what had happened to Beatrice, but he definitely liked Bebe more. And her agreeing to be his girlfriend made it all the better.

As Isaac sat there, emboldened by what had just happened, he decided to push his luck a little. "Bebe, go get me a drink."

"Okay." She popped up off the couch and took a moment to fix her dress. "Bebe will be right back." She then sashayed toward the kitchen, making sure Isaac appreciated her ass. She had no idea what kind of drink she would be able to get him, but she had a feeling she would figure it out.

As Isaac sat there, putting his cock away so that neither he nor Bebe would be tempted to try for sex again, he counted himself the luckiest man in the world. However, if Bebe was in position to think about her situation, it would be her thinking how lucky she was. In her first night as a brainless and slutty bimbo, she had already met a man who could help take care of her. Life was hard, but with someone looking out for her, she no longer needed to worry about anything. And for that she was glad. The fewer thoughts she had to have, the better.

However, while Bebe was up getting Isaac's drink, the doorbell rang. Life for Bebe and Isaac was about to get a little more complicated.

2

SPIRAL

"Oh, hi Isaac," the Clover said when the door opened to reveal Isaac inside Bebe's apartment. "I didn't realize you'd be here."

The tone that laced through Clover's voice was one of surprise and suspicion. Clover knew Beatrice was not exactly the friendly type. To have Isaac in her apartment meant something significant had changed for her neighbor.

Clover had lived next to Beatrice for as long as Beatrice had been living in the apartment building. It was a small community, but everyone knew each other, at least by name and face. Beyond that, none of them had ever shown an inkling to be friends before.

For Beatrice, the reason for never fully getting to know her neighbors was based on how much she worked and how whenever she had returned home from work, all she wanted to do was decompress and stay in. She had always been a stick in the mud, too rigid for most social situations. And that set her apart from her neighbors and other people in general.

Clover, on the other hand, was perfectly charming in

most situations, but she could be a bit free with people. She was a hippie through and through. As she stood before Isaac, she wore a tie-dyed tank top and a long flowing skirt that reached her ankles. Her feet were bare. She often walked around barefoot, preferring to maintain direct contact with the ground, keeping her closer to the Earth. It was only when she absolutely needed to that she wore sandals.

"Yeah, I was checking on Beatrice and one thing led to another," Isaac said, trying to describe the events that had just happened to him without going into detail. He still did not understand what had happened to the woman who now called herself Bebe. He knew she was Beatrice before, but Bebe was far more fun to be around. Sexier too, especially after she had just fucked him and now was doting on him.

"Yeah, I was just doing the same," Clover said, explaining her reason for ringing the doorbell. "I saw that big package earlier and then it was gone. I wanted to make sure it wasn't stolen."

"I can assure you, she got it," Isaac said.

"Hey, babe," Bebe called out with her sexy high pitched voice. "Bebe got you your drink."

Isaac tried to block the door, keeping Bebe's appearance from Clover, but it was already too late.

"Beatrice?" Clover asked. "Is that you?"

"Hi there, Clover," Bebe practically squealed. She minced over to the door in her high heels, her big tits bouncing and jiggling, barely restrained by her skimpy dress. "Bebe is so glad to see you. Do you want to see her new TV?"

Clover stood there, her mouth hanging open, trying to understand what had happened to her neighbor. There was just enough similarity between Beatrice and Bebe for Clover to connect the dots. However, she had never thought Beatrice was the type to go in for plastic surgery. And was she really talking in the third person? That was strange, but

Clover was not someone who liked to judge others. As a hippie, she tried to live a judgment free lifestyle. That was hard sometimes, but she tried nonetheless.

"Um," Clover finally said, trying to think of an answer. The truth was, Clover did not watch television. She did not even own a television. There were times she would watch a short video on her phone or on her computer—she had not completely turned her back on technology—but she had previously drawn a line about distracting herself with television.

"Oh, Bebe knows you'll love it," Bebe said. In one quick motion, she handed Isaac his drink and then grabbed Clover's wrist and pulled her into the apartment. So much had changed since Beatrice had arrived home. Her furniture had become trendy. Pink had become a major connecting color in both the decor and in Bebe's wardrobe. There was always something pink nearby.

"Sure," Clover found herself saying, not entirely sure what she was agreeing too. She was still caught up with the woman before her. Bebe had a body that looked like it came out of a porn magazine. Her big and obviously fake tits fought to escape her skimpy dress. With the blonde hair, big tits, and sparkling pink dress, she looked every bit of a bimbo. It was hard to understand what had happened to her.

Before Clover knew it, she was sitting on the couch in front of the television. Bebe had released her and started fumbling with the settings on the television. As she leaned over, she stuck her substantial ass out toward her latest guest. Bebe's dress hugged her backside tight, but it also failed to completely cover her. Clover tried not to look, but she quickly discovered that her neighbor was not wearing any panties. Then again, with a dress that tight, the lines would be ruined if she had worn panties.

"There's this cool app called Bimbo dot TV," Bebe explained. "Bebe just knows you'll love as much as her."

As soon as Bebe moved out of the way, Clover's eyes locked onto the pink spiral on the screen. It only took a moment, but suddenly she was sitting there and unable to look away. But as Bebe knew, that was only the beginning.

Clover sat there, completely transfixed by the television and the spiral on the screen. She sank deeper and deeper, fully entranced. The desire to look away left her as she gently sighed, tension leaving her body. "Pretty." It came out as a whisper, barely audible. And it was pretty. It was a pretty spiral.

As Clover sat there entranced, Bebe waved Isaac over to a chair that sat off to the side. With his drink in hand, he sat, not knowing what to expect. He had already seen what the spiral did for Bebe as she rode his cock. But unlike Clover, the spiral did nothing for him. He could look away without worry that his mind could be reprogrammed.

However, Bebe had other ideas. She instinctively knew that Isaac was not ready to go again so soon after she had drained him previously. But that did not stop her from deftly freeing his cock and wrapping her plump lips around the shaft. He might not be ready for sex again, but she could still play the role of cock sleeve, keeping his cock warm and helping it to recover as fast as possible. And by placing him off to the side, she could still see the television from the corner of her vision.

Isaac was happy to watch the screen as the Bimbo.TV app continued to show him the fun-loving and jiggly bimbos wearing bikinis on a beach somewhere. He had no idea that both Clover and Bebe saw a spiral. He had no idea that there were subliminal messages within the spiral. For Bebe, it was further cementing her bimbo personality, making sure that

Beatrice could never return. But for Clover, this was just the beginning of her indoctrination.

"I feel good."

"I love to watch the spiral."

"No thoughts are the best thoughts."

"Listen and obey."

Those were only a few of the mantras that inserted themselves into Clover's mind. She mindlessly mouthed along with them when they began to repeat. It was impossible for her to distinguish those mantras from her own voice, from her own thoughts. Her mind was a sponge, soaking up the new information at the expense of what had previously made her Clover.

The free love that Clover had lived by remained, but it became twisted with a rising interest in sex and a need to obey. The app seemed to know who it was programming and it used her own values and belief systems against her, making her want to be a sex-obsessed bimbo, just like Bebe.

When the pink glow began to pour out from the television screen and filled the room, Issac nearly jumped out of his seat. This was more than just light being emitted from the screen. The glow was almost unworldly and completely unexpected. It came from an extra component within the television set, a piece of equipment that could change the world around it.

Clover was the target of the pink light. Her body glowed with the same pink light in response. And that light kept getting brighter as her clothing melted away, disappearing from her body and leaving her completely nude.

Isaac had never seen his neighbor nude before, but he had to admit he liked what he saw. She had a fit body, even if her breasts were a little saggy. It was obvious that she went without a bra often and as a result her breasts had started to make the slow trip south.

Already above average in height, Clover did not need the height increase that Beatrice had received, but her body did become more fit and toned. And even though her breasts had started to sag a little, the increased tone of her body meant she gained a perkiness that she had long since lost.

But that was only the beginning of the changes to Clover's body. The technology from which the Bimbo.TV television set operated worked on Clover from the inside out. Her organs rearranged themselves, allowing her waist to constrict, almost making it look like she was wearing a corset. And to contrast her narrower waist, Clover's hips widened, the bones almost audibly expanding to serve as the basis of her new hourglass figure.

Matching her expanded hips was a growing ass. Clover's body shifted upward as new mass developed beneath her, a combination of new muscle and additional fat. When it was done, Clover sat upon a perfect bubble butt, big enough that nearly every man who saw her walk away would involuntarily stare. Finding pants that fit had just become a challenge.

However, the physical changes became truly noticeable when her breasts started to expand. Isaac watched with a kind of focus he had never had before. Clover's breasts shifted in shape, losing their natural teardrop shape and becoming almost perfect round, two hemispheres bolted onto her chest. Even laying on her back, they would stick straight up, giving almost no concession to gravity.

Once the new shape of Clover's breasts were created, then the growth could begin. Isaac found it difficult to watch as the pink light glowed brighter as her breasts started to expand. It was slow at first. Her skin needed time to keep up. But once her growth was properly timed with the need for more elastic skin, the growth became more and more dramatic, speeding up to a rate that should have been impossible. In any other circumstance, it would have.

Clover's breast grew into a proper set of boobs and then surpassed that by reaching the size that could best be described as tits. She had big, round, fake looking tits. Even with her expanded hips, she still looked top heavy, but that was the style from the Bimbo.TV app. Bebe was that big and now so too was Clover.

Next came more superficial changes to Clover's body. Her fingernails grew out until they reached a glamor length that would make simple tasks like typing almost impossible. But one look at her new cleavage would dissuade people from expecting her to have typing skills worth anything. The nails became colored, gaining two tones. They were mostly pink, but that pink transformed to blue at the tips. It was a different look, but one that still looked amazingly sexy.

With her nails complete, the pink glow gave her body a deep tan. Her formerly pale skin darkened as every blemish faded away. And if there was any question about tan lines, Clover now had none except for a little tan tattoo on her right hip, a peace sign to match her life as a hippie. But along with her darkening skin also came a smoothing of that same skin. Every hair on her body below the neck simply melted away, completely disappearing until she was completely bare everywhere that mattered.

It was an interesting look, Clover's tanned face on the body of a bimbo. Her dark braided hair still looked every bit like it belonged to a hippie. But that would not last. Like with the rest of her body hair, the hair on her head and face was next to disappear. Her eyebrows and eyelashes went away as her long hair was slowly reabsorbed into her head. This left her momentarily bald and very plain looking.

Before any of her hair could grow back, however, Clover's face began to transform. It started with her lips. They pushed out from her face, gaining projection before they then also gained in surface area. When they stopped growing, there was no doubt what Clover's lips were best suited for. They appeared designed to be wrapped around a cock. And even as Clover sat there, still staring at the spiral on the screen, her tongue darted out and wetted her lips, making Isaac's cock twitch in Bebe's mouth.

Once her lips were complete, Clover's nose was altered, the bump on the bridge disappearing. No other changes were needed. She already had a button nose. The final flaw had been erased. From there, it was her eyes that were made bigger.

Finally her hair started to regrow. First came her eyelashes, growing thick and long until her eyes were beautifully framed. Then came eyebrows, perfectly styled in a high arch that would give Clover a perpetually confused or surprised expression. The final change came in the hair on Clover's scalp. It grew out at a rapid pace, appearing platinum blonde instead of the dark color she had grown before. And that hair kept growing, giving her more length and volume than she had ever dreamed of before.

The original Clover put little effort and had almost no interest in her appearance. Appearing natural was what was important to her. This new Clover, however, looked more like the only thing she cared about was looking sexy. Her body appeared enhanced to an insane degree. And as pink lipstick appeared on her lips, along with blue eyeshadow, it became clear that this Clover cared deeply about looking sexy.

By the time her hair stopped growing, it nearly started to pool on the couch behind her. Long and straight, it would be difficult to deal with, but the looks she could pull off with that long hair made it more than worth it, at least in a bimbo's opinion. And Clover looked every bit like a bimbo.

That fact only became more obvious when clothing

appeared on her body. The dress she wore was pink on the top, large bands crossing her upper chest before they covered her tits, with plenty of cleavage, side boob, and under boob still visible, before it wrapped around her back and connected to her skirt. The back darkened in color until the entire skirt portion turned baby blue. The faded two-tone effect matched her nails.

The final addition to Clover as she sat there and let her mind be reprogrammed was the shoes that appeared on her feet. They were pink ankle boots that darkened to blue, just like her dress, at the sole. And that sole took up a lot of space. There was at least two inches of platform beneath her toes and the sharp heel went up at least six inches, if not higher.

However, just because Clover's body had been transformed, there were still additional changes that needed to be made. The glow from the television pulsed, flashing several times. That affected everyone in the room, even Isaac. He did not know the difference, but his cock grew a little bigger and he gained a level of stamina he had never known before, especially when it came to sex. And he too got a little extra muscle tone, something he would need if he was going to keep up with two bimbos.

But after the flashes ended, the pink glow permeated the wall and entered Clover's apartment. Her furniture and wardrobe were remade to better suit her new bimbo image. The nature art that hung on the walls turned into sexy posters of her posing in compromising positions. Clover had become a model and she was the sort of bimbo who could get off by just looking at pictures of herself.

By the time Clover's apartment had been redecorated, her mind was finally sufficiently altered. Where there had once been a smart and caring hippie, now there was just the mind of a bimbo. Fashion and sex was about all she could handle. Her mind had been reduced, her negative emotions all but eliminated, and new connections forged that meant her recollection of past events would be fuzzy at best.

When the app finished playing, the screen went dark. Bebe found herself with a mouthful of cum as Isaac grunted and shot another load into her. She savored it as she let it slide across her tongue before swallowing.

"Bebe loves cum," she announced, smacking her lips with satisfaction.

But then all eyes were on the new bimbo. Her appearance was just similar enough to her former self that it would be possible to recognize her. But that would require getting past the change in hair color and body shape. Not to mention the change in attire. The old Clover would never have considered wearing a dress like this. It was completely inappropriate and it was confining the way it wrapped so tightly around her ass. But this new woman was a bimbo and that meant her desires were different.

"Coco loves cum too," she announced, her eyes fluttering as her bimbo mind kicked into a higher gear.

Coco smiled as she spotted Isaac's cock. Even though he had just cum, he was already getting hard again, a benefit of his new stamina. His recovery time had been more than halved.

"Can Coco be your boyfriend too?" she asked. "Coco wants to share with Bebe."

That was all it took for Isaac to fully harden. He had considered himself lucky for managing to catch Bebe alone before she headed out and started fucking any guy who propositioned her. She still might. Isaac had yet to test her loyalty. But even if she did stray, Isaac had a hard time saying no to that. As long as she kept coming back, he would keep fucking her. And with Coco potentially in the picture, all the better. Isaac was definitely willing to have two bimbos at his beck and call, but it would come down to Bebe. She would be the deciding vote.

"What do you think, Bebe?" Isaac asked. As soon as the words were out of his mouth, he wondered what kind of thinking went on in her head now. She was no longer the smart and capable Beatrice. That ship had sailed. "Can Coco be my girlfriend too?"

Bebe smiled at the thought of playing with Coco. Because if both Bebe and Coco were Isaac's girlfriends, then they should get to play together as well. Bebe had never thought of herself as bisexual, but the idea of sex with a woman was no longer out of the question. And Coco was so sexy. Bebe wanted to play with Coco's tits. They could both play with each other's tits. And they could kiss and eat each other out. It was a perfect situation.

"Of course," Bebe said. "Bebe loves to share with a hot bimbo like Coco."

Coco jumped up, squealing with delight. Her tits nearly bounced out of their skimpy confines. She could not be happier.

But now that she was officially one of Isaac's girlfriends, Coco knew he needed to fuck her. Their relationship needed to be consummated, even if that was a word that was no longer in her vocabulary. The number of words available to her had been significantly reduced. But with a body like hers, no one was going to care that she could no longer remember any SAT words.

With a wide swaying of her hips, Coco walked over toward Isaac. As soon as she was in front of him, standing right next to where Bebe was still on her knees, she dropped gracefully to join her new friend. Isaac's cock was still out and Coco knew what she needed. She needed his cock.

Leaning in, Coco ran her tongue along the underside of Isaac's cock. It sprang to attention in response. The head turned purple as blood rushed into his cock once again, making his enlarged shaft hard and straight.

"Are you ready to fuck Coco now?"

Isaac did not answer with his words. He let his actions speak for themselves. He pushed himself up and turned Coco around. She was on her hands and knees as Isaac got down behind her. He barely touched her dress before the hemline sprung up over her ass, no longer able to keep her bubble butt contained.

"Fuck yes," Coco cried out as Isaac thrust his hard cock into her for the first time. The pleasure was more than Clover had ever experienced. It was like she was on some sort of sex drug, except this was no drug. This was her normal now. It was new, but oh so rewarding.

However, Coco's screams of pleasure were soon muffled when Bebe arranged herself in front of Coco, placing her pussy at just the right place where Coco could drop her head and lick.

This time it was Bebe who called out as her folds were invaded by Coco's tongue. Clover had never been talented when it came to oral sex, but Coco was a natural. Her bimbofied brain knew exactly what to do without much conscious thought. She could just react to the situation and gain pleasure from providing it.

Isaac could not believe he was fucking yet another hottie, but he was not going to deny himself this opportunity. Even if it all ended horribly, he knew he would remember this moment with fondness.

And as Bebe laid back and let herself get eaten out by her new best friend, she switched on the television again and turned the Bimbo.TV app on again. She could watch that spiral all day as it reinforced everything they had learned. Somehow, even though Coco could not see the screen as she busied herself in Bebe's pussy, she still was able to soak in the spiraling light, further reinforcing her own programming to be the best bimbo she could be.

But it was the pleasure that flowed through Coco's body that held most of her attention. Isaac's thrusts were steady, but with strength and pace that left her almost mewling each time. Her big tits jiggled and swayed beneath her, her nipples almost rubbing against the soft carpet.

Isaac was getting the hang of his newfound stamina. He found he could better control his oncoming orgasm, holding it off for as long as possible, both to maximize his fun, but to also give Coco more of what she so desperately needed. Even as she continued to lick Bebe's pussy, she still found the ability to bounce back into her boyfriend, increasing his penetration inside of her. He hit her harder and deeper than he could have otherwise.

But even a great moment such as this one needed to come to an end. "I'm cumming," Isaac roared when he could no longer hold back. His cock surged with cum. But it was not just Isaac that was cumming. His orgasm set off a chain reaction that triggered Coco's orgasm. She screamed into Bebe's pussy as her body was inundated with a torrent of erotic pleasure. Her body shook under the onslaught. But that was then enough to trigger Bebe's orgasm, all three of them cumming together in an orgasmic symphony of delight.

Coco lost all track of time as she slowly recovered from her first bimbo orgasm. Whatever fight there might have still been in her had been eradicated by the overwhelming pleasure. Even if Clover had still been in charge, she would have been second guessing herself after that, maybe even becoming addicted to such levels of pleasure. Her whole body sang with erotic delight, every fiber of her being getting in on the party.

When Coco's eyes finally fluttered open, she found herself staring at the spiral on the television screen. Her lips turned up into a smile as she simply sat there and stared, unable and unwilling to look away. She had obeyed the words that had been fed into her mind through the Bimbo.TV app and she had been rewarded for it.

However, as Isaac looked down at the two sexy bimbos who he could now both call his girlfriends, he was struck with one important question. What happened next? Was this a life they could actually live together, without repercussions or would they all need to work together to somehow maintain what they had found in each other? But that could all be figured out in the future. They had all weekend to decide what they were going to do next.

Isaac sat down on the couch. His pants had disappeared some time ago now. He did not care.

"Girls," he beckoned. "Come join me on the couch."

Without taking their eyes from the screen, Bebe and Coco rose from the floor and then sat down on either side of Isaac, snuggling up against his body, enjoying his newfound muscles. His cock started to rise again. It would not be long until he was ready to fuck again, but he still needed more time to recover. Even with his enhanced stamina, he was still only human. In the meantime, Isaac was going to enjoy watching the sexy bimbos he saw on the screen, not having any idea of the spiral that Bebe and Coco saw, further enforcing their new lives as sexy bimbos. It was all they wanted to be and Isaac was going to enjoy their future together.

3

RERUN

It was a crazy few days. Bebe and Coco loved their new lives as bimbos. Isaac enjoyed himself immensely too. He had never imagined that he could have two smoking hot and slutty bimbos at his beck and call. However, after they each had more orgasms than they could possibly count, it was time for them all to return to work.

Despite the massive changes to every one of their lives, their jobs had gone unchanged. Bebe still had the same responsibilities as Beatrice had. Coco still had the same clients she worked with as a freelance writer as she did before. The only difference was how well they could each now complete their jobs. As bimbos, work life was a lot harder. But they were both determined to succeed in their own bimbo ways.

Coco had time to let her clients down easy, that they would not be getting any writing from her, not now that the thoughts in her head that were not about sex or fashion could fill a thimble. Besides, with her long nails, typing was more than just a chore. It was nearly impossible. And the muscle memory from years spent typing had turned into a hunt and peck method that slowed Coco to a crawl, assuming she could spell the word to begin with. No amount of autocorrect could make up for her bimboish spelling.

But when it came time for Bebe to return to work, she decided it would be a good idea for Coco to join her. There was power in numbers and Bebe had already come to the conclusion that two bimbos were better than one. Even a bimbo could compute that kind of math.

However, as the pair readied themselves to visit Bebe's office, they had the hardest time figuring out what to wear. It was not that they lacked choices. Both of their closets had been remade, their wardrobes transformed to not only fit their bimbofied bodies, but to match their bimbofied style as well.

In a time like this, both bimbos would have turned to Isaac for answers. Thinking and making decisions were not their forte anymore. They needed guidance and with their polyamorous relationship with their collective boyfriend, they needed him to make the difficult decisions for them. However, after draining his balls thoroughly earlier in the morning, he had managed to separate himself from them and gotten himself off to his own job. He also needed time away to think about how he was going to make their new lives work. They did not need three apartments. Some downsizing was expected, although they both needed ample closet space to fit their expansive wardrobes.

"Is this too boring?" Bebe asked as she posed in a blouse and skirt combination that left most of her legs on display, as well as a great deal of her round tits. None of Bebe's clothes could be considered modest by conventional standards, but for a bimbo who felt it was her duty to showcase her body constantly, the concern was whether an outfit was boring or sexy. Those were the two possible grades.

But it was not just the fact the blouse highlighted the fake nature of Bebe's tits. The top was long enough where she tucked the hem into the top of her skirt. It gave her a sexy secretary look, especially with the way the skirt had a slit up the side, showing off far more of her hip than was considered work-appropriate. And still, the question was whether this particular outfit was too boring.

"Um, like, Coco thinks so," Coco answered as she chewed on a wad of gum. "You can totes go sexier."

It went back and forth like that several times. Bebe tried on outfits and Coco would eventually tell her that she could dress sexier. Not that Coco had any idea of what might be appropriate for an office environment. Not only was she now a bimbo, but the Clover of old had never worked in an office. She had never needed to dress up for work as she had always been able to work from home.

"Hmm, how about, like, this one?" Bebe asked as she posed in her latest outfit. She wore a white skirt that barely managed to cover her ass. Sitting or bending over would reveal the matching white thong she wore underneath. Her top was little more than a bikini top, also white, covering her nipples, but leaving plenty of boob still on display. The final piece to make the outfit work-appropriate was a cropped red jacket that had no hope of closing around her large tits. In every sense of common sense, this outfit was not it, but bimbos lacked common sense.

"Coco totes love it," Coco answered with enthusiasm. She bounced in place, clapping her hands, and letting her tits bounce and jiggle within the tight babydoll T-shirt she wore.

"Bebe is gonna wear it and stuff," Bebe said once she received her friend's bimbo seal of approval. "Now to, like, find the right shoes."

There was one thing that all of Bebe's massive collection of shoes had in common. They were all high heels. Even her workout shoes had a sizable heel. But that was Bebe's preference as a bimbo. The high heels helped show off her legs and ass and they forced her to stick her chest out. Not to mention they made her hips wiggle and sway as she moved. But even though high heels were known to be difficult to move in, Bebe was as graceful as a dancer when wearing them.

She finally decided on a pair of red ankle boots that matched her jacket. They were made from leather, fully encasing her feet. The spiked heel limited the stability of the shoe, but Bebe did not mind. She just loved the way they clicked and clacked as she walked across hard surfaces.

However, once Bebe was dressed, the pair walked next door to help Coco find an outfit of her own. The two bimbos were almost identical in size, so they could have easily shared Bebe's outfits, but despite them being created through the same process, the specially designed television and the Bimbo.TV app, they remained unique individuals. Bebe had a classic bimbo style, but the hippie or bohemian stylings of Clover managed to affect her bimbo sense of style as well.

It took just as long for Coco to find something to wear as it did Bebe. She tried on multiple athletes, all of them bright and colorful. In the end, the pair decided on a pink tube top that had no hope to both cover the tops of her round tits and her belly-button at the same time. The sunflower on the front stretched over her tits, but did nothing to hide the fact her hard nipples tented the fabric.

Coco's skirt featured more flowers, all of them in bright and different colors. It hugged her bubble butt like a second skin, leaving absolutely nothing to the imagination. Her yellow thong peeked out over the top. Bebe tried to persuade Coco to just go without, that a thong poking out above the top of her skirt was unprofessional, but Coco was not having it. She liked how it looked, so she kept it. And there was no way Bebe could push her friend from amping up the sexiness of the outfit.

Yellow sandals with a cork wedge heel and a thick platform beneath her toes completed the look. Like Bebe, Coco no longer owned shoes that did not feature a high heel of some sort. Although her shoes featured a large number of wedge heels so that she could more easily commune with nature. It was almost impossible to walk on sand or loose dirt with stiletto heels. This way Coco never had to think about it.

With their outfits complete, they climbed into Bebe's car, not caring that they were already late. And by the time they arrived at the office, they were even later. Even though Beatrice could have almost made the drive to work with her eyes closed, Bebe was not so lucky. She missed her exit on the freeway and then found herself driving in circles before she finally figured out where she was and what route she needed to take to reach her office building.

Coco proved to be of no help. Clover had never been a driver, not needing a car for her work. Coco had an even harder time, continually getting distracted by bright lights and shiny things. The pair were almost a hazard on the road, but they managed to avoid causing any accidents, although they did nearly drive up on a sidewalk when Coco shouted that there was a free lane. Bebe caught her bimbo friend's mistake before they jumped the curb.

However, there was one advantage to arriving more than two hours late to the office. With everyone already there, the sudden appearance of two bimbo babes walking through the building created quite a stir. The men were particularly affected, their eyes following Bebe and Coco as the pair sashayed in the general direction of Bebe's office cubicle. It was not clear what Coco could do once they arrived, since there was so little space, but Bebe had not thought that far ahead yet. And even once they arrived, she was unlikely to concern herself with such matters.

The women giggled when a delivery man dropped a package because he was too busy staring at their tits. Bebe blew kisses to the other members of her team, although everyone else was left clueless as to who she was.

As soon as Bebe and Coco arrived at Bebe's cubicle, they immediately moved to check their makeup. They dropped their purses on the desk and started rummaging through them, looking for compacts to get a better look at themselves. They completely ignored the computer on the desk and the inbox stacked high with files that Bebe was supposed to tackle upon her return to the office. She no longer had any plans to do so, because she had more important things on her mind.

"Bebe and Coco are a pair of totally sexy bimbos," Bebe said as she blew a kiss toward her reflection. She was turning herself on just by looking at herself. But that was almost expected. Both Bebe and Coco had become the ultimate pinnacle of female sexuality and all it took was a simple glance at either of their large sets of tits or their exposed skin to start getting ideas of sex. From there, it seemed normal to look at their succulent lips and imagine what those lips would feel like kissing or sucking on a clit. They both would have preferred sucking on a cock, but they could go either way.

But once their makeup was perfect, that left one major question.

"Like, what are Coco and Bebe supposed to do?" Coco asked. This was not her job. She had no idea what Bebe did for work.

"Um," Bebe started to say, filling the silence while she tried to think of an answer. Deep down, she should have been able to remember what she did for her job. But Bebe had more than just embraced being a bimbo. She consciously tried to forget about her past life. The memories were there, but she mentally chose not to access them. Beyond the information she needed to get around and to talk to people, she actively ignored everything else. And so even while she tried to think of an answer, she prevented herself from accessing the information needed to provide one.

Coco started giggling. "Bebe doesn't know, does she?"

Bebe had started the trend with speaking in the third person, treating herself as more of an object than a person, but the addition of Coco had led them both to refer to each other in the same manner. There was no "you". It was a further disassociation from their past lives.

After several long moments of silence, Bebe joined her friend in giggling before she shook her head. No words needed to be spoken. They both accepted the fact that they were dumb bimbos. Bebe was going to be useless at her job, even if she did remember what it was she was supposed to do.

However, the giggle fest was soon interrupted by the man that was Bebe's boss. "Oh good, Beatrice you're here..." His name was Joel and he trailed off as he looked up to not just see one incredibly stacked and slutty looking bimbo, but two of them. And neither of them looked like office worker material.

The women continued giggling, their eyes drifting down to Joel's crotch. They both licked their lips, imagining what was hidden away in the man's pants. When it came to men, the bimbos had a one track mind. Sex was all they cared about. And with both of them looking stunning with their stacked bodies and well highlighted assets, there were few men who could turn them down.

"Beatrice?" Joel asked in confusion. He looked from Bebe to Coco and back again, trying to understand what was going on. Neither woman looked like the Beatrice he knew.

"It's Bebe now," Bebe answered before both women

started giggling again. Once they started, it was difficult to stop.

"What happened to you?" Joel did not know what else to ask. His eyes had a hard time leaving Bebe's tits. And when he did manage to look away, they glommed onto Coco's impressive display of cleavage. With two bimbos, there was always a pair of tits to look at.

Then again, had Joel somehow managed to look Bebe in the face, she would have shimmied her shoulders to make her tits jiggle and sway or she would have simply directed his eyes back down by saying something like, "Bebe's tits are down here." With bimbos like Bebe and Coco, there was no subtlety.

"Bebe got this, like, really cool TV and stuff," Bebe started to answer. "And it's got this totally cool app called Bimbo dot TV. Bebe watched it for a while and then Bebe turned into a bimbo. Bebe got big boobies and everything. And then Bebe's neighbor came over to check on her. His name is Isaac and he's Bebe's boyfriend now. Bebe and Isaac watched the TV together while he fucked her. But then Coco came over to check on Bebe too. And she watched the Bimbo dot TV app and turned into a bimbo too. Now Bebe and Coco are both, like, Isaac's girlfriends and stuff. Isn't it great?"

Joel had a hard time following Bebe's story. It did not help that her tits kept jiggling as she talked. Even without thinking about it, her shoulders shifted back and forth, causing her tits to move, drawing Joel's focus in. But her words eventually sunk into Joel's brain, his mind processing her words. It was just slow. But the way he stared, slack-jawed, at Bebe's tits only encouraged her to play the part of a sexy bimbo even more. She had learned what worked on Isaac, but it turned out that Issac was not special in where his attention resided.

"Yeah, it's great," Joel agreed, although he found himself

distracted by the way Coco had started to compete with Bebe for his attention. It was so difficult for him to think while he had two sexy bimbos flirting with him.

"Is there someplace you can fuck Coco and Bebe?" Coco asked. She was growing more bold but also impatient. Since Bebe no longer knew what her job entailed, Coco figured that meant sex should be on the menu. And as both of them had been left wanting with Isaac's early trip to his own job, Joel would have to make up the difference.

Joel swallowed hard, beads of sweat breaking out on his forehead. It was not that he wanted to avoid fucking the pair of bimbos before him, but even he had to admit he was a little intimidated by them. They were so sexy. Their tits were so big and round. Their lips alone would have made his cock hard, the image of their lips wrapped around his cock etched into his mind. But there was something about the situation that seemed so wrong. Normal women did not transform like this in a matter of days. And yet, the proof of the situation was standing right before him, coming on to him and wanting him to do that which his cock desperately wanted.

"This way," Joel finally said, giving in to his baser instincts. He turned and led the two bimbos toward a conference room with privacy windows. The space was used when absolute secrecy was needed. It even had a back entrance for when discreet clients were brought in, avoiding the main lobby. Joel knew the room was not currently in use. He was usually in on private meetings held there, so he was aware that none were scheduled for the day. But more importantly, the room was both mostly soundproofed and the glass was frosted to prevent anyone from looking in. It was perfect to fuck the two bimbo sluts who had shown up in Beatrice's place.

Joel did not even care that Beatrice had turned into Bebe. As far as he cared, they were just a couple bimbos who wanted him to fuck them. And with his cock taking charge of his thinking, there was nothing that could stop him.

"In here ladies," Joel said as he held the door open to the two bimbos.

The path between Bebe's cubicle and the conference room had taken them by multiple other cubicles and offices. Eyes trailed the two bimbos as they swayed with each step, their bodies moving in erotica synchrony with each other, making every cock hard in a sizable radius. Even a few women found themselves growing wet at the erotic display of the two scantily clad bimbos following behind Joel.

But once the door was closed to the conference room, both bimbos knew exactly what to do. They might not have had many thoughts running through their heads anymore, but they had an instinctual understanding of how to use their bodies and how to please every cock they had access to.

Bebe and Coco both dropped to their knees as soon as the door clicked shut and Joel slid the lock closed. No one would disturb them now, or so Joel assumed. All the bimbos knew was that the click of the lock was the signal for them to begin.

Bebe shrugged off her jacket, revealing even more of her tanned skin and even more of her tits. Meanwhile, Coco reached up and freed Joel's straining cock from the confines of his slacks.

"Ooh," both bimbos cooed as they were greeted with Joel's cock for the first time. It was bigger than they had anticipated, but that only made it more enticing to them. Bebe's eyes crossed as she tried to keep it in her line of vision as she leaned forward and kissed the head with her plumped up lips. Coco followed a moment later, sharing the cock between them. They were bimbo best friends and were already used to sharing cock, since they had both decided to become Isaac's girlfriends.

"I want to fuck Bebe on the table from behind," Joel announced. "She can eat you out Coco."

Giddy, both women jumped up to their feet, their tits bouncing even more with the sudden up and down movement. It only took a moment before Bebe had pulled the bikini top from her body and pushed her big tits into the cold wood varnish of the table. She stuck out her ass and wiggled it in Joel's direction.

"I always wanted to fuck you," Joel said, thinking about how he had long wanted to remove the stick from Beatrice's ass. He thought she would have made a great lay. Little had he known that her whole world would change so dramatically, turning her into a slut for cock with a bimbo body that was designed for sex.

The height of Bebe's heels made her pussy perfectly line up with Joel's cock. The height difference was no longer an issue. Bebe giggled as she rubbed her hard nipples against the conference table. But the real giggling came when Coco climbed up onto the table. She spread her legs in front of Bebe and scooted forward until her pussy was pressed into Bebe's face. There was no escape for Bebe, not that she wanted to escape. She started licking Coco's pussy immediately, her body operating on instinct.

And that did not change when Joel thrust his hard cock deep into Bebe's pussy. She moaned into Coco sex, but did not stop her ministrations as Joel set up a steady rhythm in her velvet-like channel.

Joel had never felt a better pussy before. His cock had found the kind of home a man could only dream of. Bebe had not just been remade on the outside. Her insides had been sculpted for sex too. And now Joel was enjoying every bit of what the Bimbo.TV app had created.

Joel slapped Bebe's ass between thrusts, enjoying how her body rippled from the contact. "Yeah, spank that bimbo ass,"

Coco cheered on. But even she quickly gave into the pleasure Bebe provided her, leaning back and playing with her big tits, teasing her nipples through the thin fabric of her top. And once that started, her moans of pleasure only grew louder and more desperate.

Both bimbos were well on their way to orgasm. Their bodies had been redesigned so that even the most clumsy of hands or cock could push them to orgasm.

But it was Joel who set everything into motion. Unable to hold himself back, her cock surged with cum. A hot torrent of seed shot forth from his cock, painting Bebe's insides white. She felt the surge inside of her, which set her own orgasm into motion. Her vision went white as she came, her whole body convulsing under the onslaught of erotic pleasure. Her tongue grew more active as she continued to lick Coco's pussy and clit.

But that frantic mouth work was then what pushed Coco over the edge as well. Soon both bimbos were screaming out as erotic energy coursed through their bodies, lighting up every fiber of their being with pleasure. Their orgasmic screams even pushed the soundproofing of the room to the limit. There was a point where even the noise canceling technology employed in the room reached its limit. The conference room had simply not been designed to block out such screams.

Joel felt himself nearly collapse against the conference table as he pulled out of Bebe's tight pussy. A string of cum still connected her wet folds and the head of his cock, their juices intermingling. He had never had sex like that before. His partners had always been of the long and loving variety. He had never really fucked a woman like that where he had only cared about his own pleasure, going at whatever pace he wanted, behaving almost animalistic in her fervor.

But while he supported himself against the table, catching

his breath, he failed to hear the click of the door lock. Joel was not the only person in the building with the key to the conference room.

The door swung open and the voice of a woman entered the room. "Go find Joel. He'll want to be in on this meeting."

But then the woman looked up. She saw the scene that had just unfolded. She saw Bebe with her skirt pushed up over her hips. She saw the short red jacket discarded on the floor, as well as the bikini top pushed off to the side. She saw the other blonde woman, Coco, sitting on the conference table, her pussy completely exposed and on display. And then she spotted Joel, his pants around his ankles, his spent cock hanging there.

"Never mind, Simon," the woman said. "It turns out he's right here and about to be fired."

The woman walked into the room and the man she had been speaking to, Simon, followed her in. The woman was Annika Roach, the newly appointed CEO. She had appointed herself to that position after buying out the company. Simon was her second in command. Both were new to the company, but Annika was intent on placing her mark on the company.

She narrowed her eyes at Joel. His mind was moving slowly after his orgasm. It was only just starting to sink in that they were no longer alone.

"Hi, my name is Coco," Coco said cheerily. "And this is Bebe."

Bebe turned her head and smiled at the newcomers. She winked at Simon.

"What the hell is going on in here?" Annika demanded. "Joel, who are these women? Are the prostitutes? They don't work here, do they?"

"Bebe does," Bebe spoke up. "But she doesn't remember what her job is anymore and stuff."

"I can explain," Joel finally said, hoping he could salvage

his job. "Bebe used to be Beatrice. But then an app turned her into a bimbo. She brought her friend to work today. I don't know why. But they dragged me in here and made me…" Joel was unable to finish speaking. His mind was only operating at half speed and he had run out of lies that could possibly save his job. He had not been dragged into the conference room. It had been his suggestion to use the room to fuck in.

"Simon and I were going to include you on some of the cuts we want to make, but I guess we can already eliminate a few positions. Joel, you're fired."

"But—"

"And it's Bebe, is it?" Annika continued, ignoring Joel's protests. "Or Beatrice or whatever you want to call yourself? Since you supposedly work here, you're fired too. And you, Coco or whatever, if you don't work here you can get the fuck out of here. All three of you. I want you gone in fifteen minutes."

And just like that, Bebe was out of a job. Not that she minded. Any job that did not let her fuck on the job was not a job that she wanted to keep. She was a sexy bimbo, not a worker drone. Her value was in her body, not her mind and certainly not in any other skill beyond being the sexiest bimbo around.

Bebe and Coco needed little time to actually put their outfits back together. Bebe needed a little time to put her bikini top and jacket back on, but Coco was able to help with that as soon as she pulled her skirt back down over her ass.

Joel pulled up his pants, but no matter what he did, he looked disheveled and sad. He had lost his job and he had no idea what to do with himself now. His only consolation was that he had gotten fired for having the best sex of his life. That counted for something.

Bebe and Coco left the building, arm in arm, practically skipping in their high heels as they made their way toward

Bebe's car. Eyes followed them as they went, creating a blip in the efficiency of the entire company workforce. They were a distraction to everyone everywhere that they went. But Bebe and Coco would not have had it any other way. They loved to be the center of attention.

"Joel, wait up," Simon called out as Joel left the building five minutes later, carrying a box of his personal items from his office.

Joel stopped and turned, surprised to see Simon chase after him. He had expected to be ostracized by everyone in management following Annika's clear disapproval of his actions and his public firing. Everyone in the company was made aware of what Joel had done.

"That was really Beatrice?" Simon asked. Simon had been aware of Beatrice before, but only in passing. He had seen her as a hard worker, but completely plain in every other way.

"She goes by Bebe now."

"But what happened to her?" Simon pressed. "She wasn't always like that, was she?"

Joel shrugged his shoulders. He did not even know why he was sharing this information with Simon. Maybe it was that the whole day had seemed so improbable. "Apparently there was some app that turned her into a bimbo. I don't know how it works and I don't even remember what it was called. Whatever it was, it got me fired, so if you don't mind, I'm going to go find a bar and get drunk. I have no idea what I'm going to do now."

"Look, man, I'm sorry," Simon said. "I can't blame you for what you did. Maybe this can help soften the blow. I've got a friend who's hiring. I'll put in a good word for you."

Simon placed a card belonging to his friend in Joel's box and then waved goodbye. Simon returned to his job and Joel headed toward his car, his head hanging low. Even with the promise of a possible job, he was still down, knowing that he had just screwed up his future.

Meanwhile, since Bebe and Coco were done with work early, they decided to head to the mall for some shopping. That was the sort of thing bimbos did when they had free time. And both of them were excited to model and then buy some new and sexy clothing.

However, back inside the building, Simon was starting to make a plan. Seeing what had happened to Beatrice, turning into Bebe, had given him an idea. Simon had always been in Annika's shadow. But with the right plan, he might be able to find his own light while giving his boss something else to live for. If Beatrice could turn into a sexy bimbo, why couldn't Annika?

* * *

Annika and Simon will return in a future series.

ABOUT THE AUTHOR

Sadie Thatcher is a longtime author of erotic fiction, especially related to transformations and bimbofication. She likes to say "I have thrown off the shackles of my conservative upbringing and now write erotic stories."

She maintains a special blog devoted to her writings, including a behind the scenes look at her writing process, and bimbos in general, as well as highlights works by other authors. They can be found at:

https://authorsadiethatcher.tumblr.com

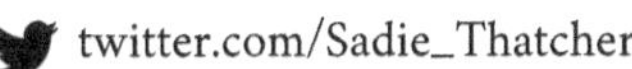 twitter.com/Sadie_Thatcher

ALSO BY SADIE THATCHER

Tales from the Bimbo Ward: Tegan

Tales from the Bimbo Ward: Susan

Tales from the Bimbo Ward: Joy

Tales from the Bimbo Ward: Katherine

Tales from the Bimbo Ward: Sarah

Tales from the Bimbo Ward: Salt and Pepper

Tales from the Bimbo Ward: Amanda

Tales from the Bimbo Ward: The Staff

Mistaken Identity

My New Bimbo Life

Keep Calm and Be a Good Bimbo

(Virtual) Reality

Side Effects

Plaything of Olympus

Experiment in Submission

Bimbo Bet

Snow White and the Evil Witch

Twelve Days of Bimbo

Chosen

The Faerie's Gift

The Bimbo in Yellow

Bad Role Model

Truth or Bimbo

Truth or Bimbo College Edition

Bimbo Dome

Acting the Part

Subliminal Society

Inheritance

Company Morale

His Bimbo Girlfriend

The Bimbo Room

The Bimbos of Blossom

Dr. Jekyll and Missy Hyde

Second Chance

From M&As To T&A

Trading Places

The Bimbo Nutcracker Suite

Milked and Herded

Fitting In

Clowning Around

Transformative Ink

Choices

Rival Competition

Alien Womanhood

Invasion

The Princess and the Bimbo

Bimbo Labyrinth

The Legend of the Werebimbo

Power and Corruption

The Simulation

The Curse of Playing Bimbo Tag

The Curse of Playing Bimbo Tag: Jenna or Jenni

The Bimbo Professor: The Curse of Playing Bimbo Tag Book 3

Anything for the Job

Anything for the Job 2

Anything for His Job

The Bimbo in the Mirror

The Bimbo in the Mirror 2

Astrid and the Bimbo Bee

Bella and the Bimbo Bee

Cali and the Bimbo Bee

Desiree and the Bimbo Bee

Ember and the Bimbo Bee

Fiona and the Bimbo Bee

The Intern

The Lawyer

The Hacker

Cause & Effect

Witless Protection

Stealing Sally

Trial and Error

Beta Testing

Exposed

Bimbo for a Weekend

Bimbo for a Week

Bimbo for Life

Fake It Until You Make It Season 1

Fake It Until You Make It Season 2

Simple and Fun Volume 1

Simple and Fun Volume 2

Simple and Fun Volume 3

Simple and Fun Volume 4

Simple and Fun Volume 5

Simple and Fun Volume 6

Bimbo Halloween

Bimbo Christmas

Bimbo Technology

Dorm Room Bimbo

Carissa's Magic Pen

Spirit Walk

Muscle Memory

The Case of the Bimbo Wife

Changes

Changes 2

New Year New You

The Bimbo Dream

The Wedding Gift

The Cure

Backfire

Bim & Bo Yoga

Wishing for Each Other

Bimbo Roots

A Bimbo at Oktoberfest

The Lost Bet

The Fountain

Bimbo Ghost

Sugar and Spice and Everything Nice

Basic Bimbo

Body Swap Rings 2: Wedding Night

The Bimbo Experience

The Bimbo Experience 2

The Bimbo Experience 3some

The 4th Bimbo Experience

Bimbo Genes

Bimbo Genes II: The Virus

The Bimbo Genes III: The Epidemic

Bimbo Juice: Blue Raspberry

Bimbo Juice: Grape

Bimbo Juice: Mango

Bimbo Juice: Pineapple

Bimbo Juice: Red Apple

Bimbo Juice: Veggie

Bimbo Juice Gone Wild: The Muse

Bimbo Juice Gone Wild: Street Racer

Bimbo Juice Gone Wild: Score

Bimbos of the Traveling Earrings: Book 1

Bimbos of the Traveling Earrings: Book 2

Bimbos of the Traveling Earrings: Book 3

Bimbos of the Traveling Earrings: Book 4

Bimbo Party: Kennedy

Bimbo Party: Esme

Bimbo Party: Ariana

Bimbo Party: Tara

Workout Buddies

Wishful Thinking

Wanting More

Bimbo Harem: Annabelle

Bimbo Harem: Josie

Bimbo Harem: Nikki

Bimbo Harem: Tiana

Giggle Dust

Giggle Dust 2.0

Giggle Dust 3.0

Giggle Dust 4.0

Bimbo Takeover: The First Step

Bimbo Takeover: Teammates

Bimbo Takeover: Going to the Top

Bimbo Takeover: Revenge of the Bimbos

Thanks for the Mammaries

A New Beginning

Copying Kat

Spreading the Love

Discovering Eden

Building Eden

Spring In Eden

Saving Eden

The Perfect Girlfriend

The Perfect Engagement

The Perfect Wife

The Perfect Woman

Be Hot, Not Smart

No Thoughts for Thots

Be Art, Not Smart

The Cream of the Crop